FLYING FERGUS

The Big Biscuit Bike Off

CHRIS HOY

with Joanna Nadin

Illustrations by Clare Elsom

First published in Great Britain in 2016 by
Piccadilly Press
80-81 Wimpole St, London W1G 9RE
www.piccadillypress.co.uk

Copyright © Sir Chris Hoy, 2016

This is a work of fiction. Names, places, events and incidents are either the
products of the author's imagination or used fictitiously. Any resemblance to
actual persons, living or dead, or actual events is purely coincidental.

A CIP catalogue record for this book is available from the British Library.

ISBN: 978–1–471–40523–5
also available as an ebook

3 5 7 9 10 8 6 4

Typeset in Berkeley Oldstyle
Printed and bound by Clays Ltd, St Ives Plc

Piccadilly Press is an imprint of Bonnier Zaffre,
a Bonnier Publishing company
www.bonnierpublishingfiction.co.uk
www.bonnierpublishing.co.uk

Meet Fergus
and his friends...

Chimp

Fergus

Grandpa Herc

Mum

Daisy

Jambo Patterson

Calamity Coogan

Minnie McLeod

Belinda Bruce

Wesley Wallace

Dermot Eggs

Choppy Wallace

Mikey McLeod

. . .and see where they live

Fergus's house

Daisy's house

Grandpa's junk shop

NAPIER STREET

Bandstand

Play park

CARNOUSTIE COMMON

Bruce's Biscuits

Prince Waldorf

Dimmock

Demelza

Hounds of Horribleness

Meet Princess Lily
and her friends...

Princess Lily

Suet

Unlucky Luke

Douglas

...and explore Nevermore

The Big Idea

Fergus Hamilton was an ordinary nine-year-old boy. He liked fairground rides (but not the really scary ones), spicy sauces (but not the triple chilli ones), and his dog Chimp (but not when he'd rolled in fox poo, which was quite often). He didn't like cod liver oil (but he swallowed it), or homework (but he did it), or the way his mum sometimes called him "Fergie-Wergie" in front of his best friend Daisy (but he didn't say anything).

Yes, he was ordinary in almost every way, except one. Because, for a small boy, Fergus Hamilton had an extraordinarily big imagination.

Some days he imagined Chimp was the fastest pure-bred greyhound in the world, instead of being a rescued mongrel who only sped up if there was a sausage involved.

Some days he imagined he was a government spy, living in a string of glamorous hotels, instead of a schoolboy living in the flat above his grandpa's second-hand bike shop on Napier Street. Though at least Herc's Hand-Me-Downs was better than the junk shop it had been until a few weeks ago. Selling second-hand bikes was way more interesting than selling – or not selling – broken washing machines and old tin trays.

Some days he imagined his dad lived with them, instead of in Kilmarnock, which was where Mum said he was, or in a parallel universe called Nevermore, which was where Fergus was sure his dad was. All he had to do to get there was get up to speed on his bike and let the pedals spin backwards three times and he could land wherever in Nevermore he wanted. Next time Fergus went he was going to start hunting for his dad straight away. But not right now. Right now he had another dream to concentrate on.

As he pedalled faster and faster, Fergus was imagining that he was zooming around Middlebank stadium, taking the lead in the District Championships, cheered on by none other than Steve "Spokes" Sullivan, champion cyclist, world record-holder and the brains behind the Sullivan Swift, the bike of Fergus's dreams. If Fergus had his way he'd get the newest model, the Swift Elite, in "super scarlet" with yellow detailing, to match his cycling kit, which was also imaginary. Yes, Fergus could see it all in his head now, the bright red and custardy colours blurring into orange as he whizzed past the commentators' box and headed up the home straight, the finishing line just seconds away! All he had to do was keep his eyes on the prize, that's what Grandpa said. Eyes on the . . .

WHOMP! Fergus was brought back down to earth, literally, as his front wheel hit a massive tussock, sending him flying over the handlebars and into a heap at the foot of the bandstand. Because of course Fergus wasn't at Middlebank, he was on Carnoustie Common, and he wasn't riding a Swift Elite or wearing a fancy new red and yellow Lycra kit, he was in old blue jeans and trainers on his second-hand bike.

Or, rather, off it.

Fergus sighed as he pulled himself and his bicycle upright again. *This is ridiculous*, he thought. There was no way he or any of his team – the Hercules' Hopefuls – were going to get their speeds up if the only place they had to practise was the park; swerving in and out of dogs and small children and Mrs MacCafferty from two doors down. Worst of all, he wasn't alone in his thoughts.

"Unlucky, Hamilton," said a voice from above.

Fergus knew exactly who it was before he even looked up. There, leaning over the railing of the bandstand and flanked by his sidekick Dermot Eggs, stood the number one racer on Wallace's Winners, and Fergus's number one enemy: Wesley Wallace.

"What do you want, Wesley?" Fergus asked.

"Oh, just to see how easily I'm going to beat you," said Wesley. "That's all."

"Yeah, that's all," echoed Dermot, who rarely had anything of his own to say.

"It was an accident," said Fergus. "It could have happened to anyone."

Wesley smiled thinly. "Well, anyone who has to cycle in a kiddies' park," he scoffed. "You wouldn't catch that sort of thing happening to any of us down at Middlebank."

Fergus didn't bother to reply. He

knew it was true, and he knew it was unfair as well. Why should Wallace's Winners get to train at Middlebank? Why should they be the ones to get a sleek new kit every season, sponsored by Bruce's Biscuits? Why should they all get a discount on new bikes from Choppy Wallace's shop whenever they wanted? Of course they were going to win the Districts; they'd win everything with advantages like that. And with those cross thoughts banging around in his brain, Fergus rode slowly and sulkily home.

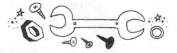

Fergus still hadn't shaken the bad mood by the time he burst back through the door of the shop.

"It's not fair!" he said to no one in particular.

Chimp looked up from the inner tube he was trying to kill (thinking it might be a snake of some sort).

Grandpa looked up from the inner tube he was trying to revive with his puncture repair kit. "What's not fair, sonny?" he asked.

"Oh . . . EVERYTHING," snapped Fergus, sulkily. Then, remembering it was Grandpa he was talking to, not Wesley, he softened his voice. "It's just that I fell off. Again."

"Och, Fergie." Grandpa smiled. "If you don't crash on a regular basis you've got to ask yourself if you're trying hard enough."

"It's not that," said Fergus. "I don't mind falling off when it's because I'm going too fast, or too slow, or because I slip on the pedals. But I do mind when it's because no one's mown the grass for months or someone's dropped litter. And I bet Spokes Sullivan never dropped out of a race because Colin the cat got in the way again."

Chimp whimpered at the mention of his own arch-nemesis and buried his head between his paws.

"Here," said Grandpa, holding out a plate of marmalade sandwiches. "I made your favourite."

Fergus took one, but he still couldn't crack a smile, not even with his mouth full of sweet, chewy orange peel.

"Listen, I know it's not fair," continued Grandpa. "Life's not fair. If it was, we'd all be living in palaces and riding around on hovermobiles. And this shop would be on Princess Street with a fleet of shop assistants instead of a dog who chews half my stock."

Fergus felt the corners of his mouth twitch as he glanced down at Chimp who, having destroyed the would-be snake, was now gazing with intent at a bicycle pump. He quickly held out a crust to Chimp instead as Grandpa finished what he had to say.

"The point is we just have to work hard. Some of us a lot harder than others."

"But we could work all day and night and still never be as good as Wesley Wallace and his lot," said Fergus. "Not without a proper track."

Grandpa nodded thoughtfully. "True, true."

"So what do we do?" demanded Fergus. "The Districts are only eight weeks away."

"I know," said Grandpa. "I'm thinking. Give a man a minute to exercise the old grey matter."

So Fergus did. He counted down from sixty seconds, waiting and hoping for a big idea.

Forty-two . . .

"Ooh," said Grandpa. Then, "No, that won't work."

Fergus held his breath.

Twenty-nine . . .

"We could . . . no, we couldn't."

Fergus felt his heart flip and flop inside him like a floundering fish. Another ten seconds passed. Then they were down to nine. And eight. Seven. Six.

Five . . .

"We could . . . "

Fergus's heart seemed to hold as still as his breath

Four . . .

"Maybe…"

Three . . .

"Or definitely…"

Two . . .

"Yes. I've really . . ."

One . . .

"GOT IT!" Grandpa said.

Fergus let out an enormous burst of air. "What is it?" he cried, Chimp leaping and barking around his feet at the excitement. "What are we going to do?"

Grandpa winked. "That, sonny, is for me to know and for you to find out."

"Huh?"

"You heard," Grandpa said. "Tomorrow, all will become clear. But right now I've got work to do. And so have you. Your mam'll be up for work any minute and there's homework to do and potatoes to peel so I'd get a shimmy on if you know what's good for you."

Fergus did know what was good for him, because if the potatoes didn't get peeled he'd only have to eat the skins as well, which he'd really rather not. But as he dunked another spud in the sink, his felt his heart plummet with it. "What kind of plan's going to win us the Districts, eh, Chimp?"

Chimp sighed and dropped his head onto his paws.

"My thoughts exactly," said Fergus, despondently. "We haven't a hope, whatever Grandpa reckons. Not a single hope."

The City Council

"We're doing what?" asked Fergus, looking up at the grey, gloomy City Council building.

"I told you," Grandpa said. "We're going to see the parks manager, Mr McGovern. He's an old friend of mine."

"We're going to tell him to sort out the common," added Daisy, who had come along for moral support, and because an afternoon out at the council was better than one in with all her mum's rules and regulations. In fact, Mum would have made a pretty good council boss, Daisy reckoned, although she was pretty sure her mum would have had everyone wearing safety helmets just to walk to school. And as for a new cycle track? Not unless it was made of cotton wool with bubble wrap lining the sides.

"We're going to ask him, Daisy, not 'tell him'," Grandpa pointed out. "We can't make the council do anything they don't want to."

Daisy harrumphed. "More's the pity. I'd tell them to ban dog poo. And build a bigger slide because the one we've got isn't nearly scary enough. Oh – and free ice lollies for all children on really hot days."

Chimp barked.

"And for dogs, too," said Daisy quickly.

Grandpa laughed. "Well, we can save those battles for another day. Right now we've got to focus on one thing and one thing only."

"They'll never build a proper track, though," said Fergus, before adding a hopeful, "Will they?"

"Well, that's what we're here to find out," said Grandpa. "So suits straight and best smiles on, and let some hope into your hearts, eh?"

Fergus looked down at his scuffed trainers and grass-stained knees. Well, he could maybe manage the last two anyway, and so he forced his face into a smile and crossed his fingers as the foursome marched up the steps.

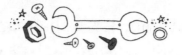

"Herc!" said a broad man wearing a tweed suit, a red tie and an even redder face.

"Malky!" Grandpa held out his hand and the other man took it and shook it so hard Fergus thought he might snap it off.

"Long time, no see," said Mr McGovern. "How are things over at Napier Street? I hear you've given up on junk and you're in the bike business now."

"You hear right," said Grandpa. "Got my own shop and cycling team, too. And these pair are two of my top racers."

Fergus felt pride and embarrassment flush his face until it was as red as Mr McGovern's.

"So I'm told," said the man himself. He nodded at Daisy and Fergus. "I've heard a lot about you."

"Who from?" asked Daisy.

"Och, I saw Jambo Patterson's piece in the paper. He seems to like you lot, and he's got a nose for these things. If Jambo's excited, I'm excited!" exclaimed Mr McGovern. "You're going to have Wallace's Winners on the hop though, I'll bet."

"Well, that's what we came about," blurted Fergus, then hastily looked at Grandpa to check it was okay.

Grandpa nodded at him to go on.

"The thing is," Fergus continued, "if we ARE going to beat Wallace's Winners at the District Championships, we need a better track. So –"

"So if you could just build one on Carnoustie Common for us that would be BEAST!" interrupted Daisy, before adding a hurried, "Please, Mr McGovern," at the end.

Mr McGovern smiled but didn't say anything, then looked down at his desk for a minute.

Maybe he was just thinking, like Grandpa had been, thought Fergus. *Working out how much money they could have and who would do the work. Yes, that would be it. Bound to be.*

But . . .

"I'm sorry," Mr McGovern said finally, shaking his head. "Thing is, the council just don't have the cash. Not only that, but I'm not sure we've got Carnoustie Common for much longer either. It's been earmarked for an extension for Bruce's Biscuits – they're willing to pay good money for the land because they want to build a digestive wing."

"Digestives?" cried Daisy, even though she was as big a fan of biscuits as she was of biking. "But that's unbelievable!"

"Unfathomable!" agreed Grandpa.

"Unfair," insisted Fergus quietly. "That's what it is, unfair."

Mr McGovern shrugged. "Och, you're not wrong, sonny. It's unfair and then some. But it's out of my hands. The council needs the money. And besides, I know you're keen on it, but how many other people use that park, hey?"

Fergus sighed and Daisy slumped.

But Grandpa leaned over the desk. "I think you'd be surprised."

"I think I would too," said Mr McGovern.

"Then prepare to be amazed," said Grandpa.

Mr McGovern leaned back in his chair and let his mouth slip into a small smile. "What have you got up your sleeve, eh, Herc?"

"Oh . . . just an inkling of an idea, Malky," said Grandpa. "A wee plan."

"It had better be better than the last one," muttered Fergus, but Daisy nudged him to shut up so he did.

As soon as they were back outside, though, he was pestering Grandpa with questions. "Is it a celebrity?" he asked. "Are we going to get Johnny Sparkle to do a concert?"

"Ugh," said Daisy, who hated Johnny Sparkle's songs. "How about the Crazy Classix Choir? They can gargle the whole of Beethoven's Fifth Symphony."

"Or . . ." Fergus had a better idea ". . . Spokes Sullivan! Is that it? Are you going to ask Spokes to pay for the park? I bet he would. He must have the money now he's won the World Championships!"

"It's not Johnny Sparkle, it's not Spokes and it's not anyone who can gargle or burp a symphony or even play it on a pair of spoons!" said Grandpa. "By jinks, not everything has to come down to celebrities."

"I know," said Fergus quietly. "But . . . what then?"

"Never you mind," said Grandpa, tapping the side of his nose. "You two concentrate on the cycling. I'll concentrate on everything else."

But Fergus couldn't concentrate. He couldn't concentrate at all. At tea he kept dropping his chips on the floor, which drove Mum potty but pleased Chimp no end. At team practice Minnie McLeod tried to teach him to bunny hop on her BMX but his legs were so shaky he looked more like their accident-prone teammate Calamity Coogan. And late that night in bed, while Chimp snored happily at his side dreaming of sausages, Fergus could only toss and turn, his brain still fizzing with thoughts about what Grandpa might be up to.

"It *has* to be Spokes," he said to himself. "It just HAS to be." Despite what Grandpa had said about celebrities, he felt sure it was going to be his hero who saved the day. Fergus imagined the look on everyone's faces when Spokes showed up with an enormous cheque, and the look on Wesley Wallace's face when Fergus and his friends had the best cycle track in the whole of Scotland.

And with that happy picture in his head, Fergus finally fell asleep.

Bikes or Biscuits?

By Saturday afternoon, though, Fergus was beginning to have his doubts again. Not only was he two seconds slower on each lap, but Grandpa was refusing to fess up to anything.

"Please tell us," Fergus begged, after he'd come a cropper on a tussock for the third time in as many minutes.

"Yes, go on, Mr H," pleaded Daisy, who was beginning to get a tad tired of having to take detours around puddles, fizzy drink cans and Chimp, who had taken a fancy to a patch of their circuit as a likely place for buried bones.

"Patience, grasshoppers, patience," said Grandpa mysteriously.

But Fergus wasn't feeling very patient, so when there was still no news by teatime, he couldn't keep his gloomy thoughts to himself any longer.

"I don't think there IS a plan," he said as Mum plopped some fishfingers onto his plate.

"Don't talk daft," Mum replied. "Your grandpa's always got a trick up his sleeve, haven't you, Herc?"

Grandpa lowered his copy of the *Evening News*, and had a quick check inside the arms of his shirt. "Yup," he said, "definitely something up there."

"Oh, ha ha," said Fergus. "Very funny."

"Well, if you're wanting serious," said

Grandpa, "have a read of this." And he passed the paper to Fergus. "Something that might interest you in there."

"Och, Herc, it's teatime, can't it wait?" complained Mum.

"I think he's waited long enough," said Grandpa. "Besides, cold fishfingers are fit for a king."

Fergus did agree with that, but he was still gloomy and it was with a heavy heart that he picked up the paper and started flicking through the pages.

CARNOUSTIE PAIR IN CRIME CAHOOT!

read one headline.

"Nope, can't be that," thought Fergus, because he definitely hadn't been in any crime cahoot that he knew of, unless it was secretly slipping Chimp his helping of neeps last Wednesday. He turned to page two.

WALLACE WINS AGAIN!

exclaimed an article on Choppy's prize for "local business of the year".

Fergus felt himself bristle with anger. "Do you really think I want to read this?" he demanded.

"That? Oh, ignore that, sonny," said Grandpa. "Have a look at the next page."

Fergus sighed heavily, but did as he was told and read the headline on page three. Then he read it again to be sure. Then a third time for good measure. But it still said the same thing – the same unbelievable thing:

BISCUITS OR BIKES?

it asked in big, bold letters. Underneath was a whole page all about the park and how Bruce's Biscuits were going to buy it and plough it up to make room for a bigger factory. Then came the best bit: a photo of Fergus and his friends after getting through to the Districts, and a plea to readers to do anything they could to "keep Hercules' Hopefuls on track for the future".

"I . . ." began Fergus, but for once he seemed lost for words. "You . . ." he tried again.

"I think 'Thanks, Grandpa' is what

BISCUITS OR BIKES?

Report by James 'Jambo' Paterson

Carnoustie Common could soon be covered in concrete following Bruce's Biscuits' announcement that they want the park for a brand new digestive wing.

The biscuit baron Brian Bruce has earmarked land taking in as much as a third of Carnoustie Common, including the bandstand and the children's play area. The common is used daily by District Championship cycle contenders Hercules' Hopefuls. Fresh from their second placing in the Great Cycle Challenge, the young team had high hopes for this season, but this is a real setback. If you can do anything to help their cause, contact us here at the paper or the team coach Hercules Hamilton at Herc's Hand-Me-Downs on Napier Street, and help keep Hercules' Hopefuls on track for the future.

you're looking for," said Grandpa.

Fergus nodded furiously. "B– But . . . how?" he managed to stutter.

"Check the byline," said Grandpa.

Fergus found the name of reporter at the top of the page, and felt everything slide into place in his head. "Jambo Patterson!" he said.

"Jambo?" asked Mum. "The reporter who congratulated you after the Great Cycle Challenge?"

"The very same," said Grandpa. "He's a big fan of Fergie, and of the park, so he said he'd do whatever he could to help out, and this is proof he's true to his word."

"So what happens now?" asked Fergus.

"Well, that's the downside," said Grandpa. "You're going to need to be a little more patient."

Fergus rolled his eyes. He was beginning to lose his patience with patience.

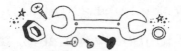

This time, though, he didn't have to wait too long to find out what was going to happen next. The first envelope plopped onto the doormat within the hour, addressed to Grandpa.

"What is it?" Fergus asked.

"Here," said Grandpa, holding it out to him. "Open it and see."

Fergus did as he was told, sliding a finger under the seal and slitting it to reveal a crisp twenty-pound note inside, along with a postcard from Mr Osborne at Number 47 saying "To my old pal, Herc – good luck."

"Wow!" said Fergus.

"Big money may do most of the talking, Fergie, but community spirit is still pretty strong round here," said Grandpa. "Mr Osborne may be the first, but he won't be the last."

And he wasn't. One by one, more and more envelopes slipped through the letterbox, with notes and coins and letters of encouragement inside. And it didn't stop that night either. All through the week the money kept coming in from bake sales and piggy banks and sponsored you-name-its; people even dropped by the shop to fling their loose coins into a jar on the counter. And, much more importantly, they all signed the petition Fergus and Daisy had drawn up too.

"Great idea," they all said. "Keep up the good work, Herc!"

"Oh, I intend to," Grandpa always replied.

By the following Thursday Fergus and Daisy counted (three times to be sure) a total of seven hundred and ninety-eight signatures and nearly as many pounds too.

"This is BEAST!" said Daisy.

"It's . . . it's . . . BRILLIOTIC!" agreed Fergus, making up a new word because no real ones seemed to be good enough.

"It's, well, it's almost there," said Grandpa. "We'll never match what Bruce's Biscuits is offering to pay for the common. But I reckon if we can make it to a thousand names, we could show them what this community really wants."

"Aye, a park," said Fergus. "Not a packet of ginger snaps."

"But the deadline's tomorrow," wailed Daisy. "Or Bruce's Biscuits gets the land. Mr McGovern was in the paper saying so."

Fergus felt his tummy turn as cold as those fishfingers. "I thought Mr McGovern was on our side?"

"He is," said Grandpa. "But he's battling the big boys, so he has to stick to the rules. Anyway, I've not given up hope. Not yet."

"Nor me," said Daisy.

"Or me," said Fergus.

"Well, more fools you, then."

Fergus turned round to see a sneering Wesley Wallace standing in the shop doorway, together with his idiotic sidekick Dermot Eggs.

"What do you want?" he demanded.

"Oh, only to see just how pathetic your efforts are." Wesley picked up the petition. "It's a piece of paper. That's all. Everyone knows it's money that really talks round here. And I don't mean a few coins in a jar."

"Well, you'd know all about that," snapped Daisy. "You're only number one because your daddy's paid for fancy wheels."

Wesley's face reddened. "You're just jealous," he spat.

"Yeah, jealous," echoed Dermot.

"Of you two dimwits?" said Fergus. "I don't think so."

"That's enough," said Grandpa.

But Wesley hadn't finished. "You'll be the dimwits when you've got no track to practice on at all," he sneered.

Even Grandpa was riled now. "We'll see about that," he said.

"Want to bet?" taunted Wesley.

"Yes!" said Fergus, before Grandpa could say something else. "Yes I do. I bet we'll save the park by tomorrow. And then . . . then we'll build a track, a proper one, and then I bet that I beat you on it."

"No chance," said Wesley. "But I accept the bet. And let's make it REALLY interesting. Loser buys the winner ice cream from Vanoli's for a month."

"Deal!" replied Fergus, excited at the thought of a triple whip with sprinkles.

"Hang on there a mo, sonny," interrupted Grandpa.

"Too late," said Wesley, grabbing Fergus's hand. "We've shaken on it."

And with that he and Dermot stalked happily out of the shop.

"Blimey, Fergus," said Daisy. "That's done it."

Fergus shook his head. "We can do it. I know we can. I just need . . ."

"A headcheck?" suggested Grandpa.

"A fake-signature-writing machine!" suggested Daisy. "That'd be BEAST!"

"But also illegal," said Grandpa. "If we do this, we do it fair and square."

"We will," said Fergus. "I'll make sure of that." And he grabbed his own helmet off the hook on the back of the door.

"Where are you going?" asked Daisy.

"Like I was trying to say, I just need to see a man about a dog."

Chimp barked happily when he heard that word.

"Come on, boy," said Fergus. "We've got work to do."

"I'll come too," offered Daisy eagerly.

Fergus shook his head. "Not this time," he said. *Not where I'm going*, he added to himself.

Daisy shrugged. "Well, come back soon, at least."

"I will," Fergus said. And with that he headed out to the alley where his bike was kept, jumped in the saddle and set off, Chimp bounding after him. He was going straight to Nevermore to find his dad, bring him back and get him to save the day. If he could find him, that is.

"You know the drill, don't you, boy?" he yelled when they were out of eyesight and finally up to speed.

Chimp barked happily.

"Then brace yourself!"

Fergus thought about the rendezvous point he and Lily had planned: Unlucky Luke's house. He had no idea what it looked like, or where it was, but Lily had said this was down to him and his imagination, so he thought about what sort of strange place a not-so-good-at-their-job magician would live in. And what he imagined was pretty strange indeed.

"This had better work," Fergus muttered. Then he closed his eyes, let his feet back-pedal once, twice, three times . . .

Unlucky Luke's House

SWOOSH!

Fergus skidded to a halt outside what looked like a cross between a gingerbread house and a badly-gone-wrong science experiment. The chimney stuck out of the wall, the windows were hazy with multicoloured dust and on the doorstep was a strange stone animal that was half monkey, half vicious-looking bird.

"Don't much fancy the look of that critter," growled Chimp.

"Nor me," admitted Fergus, happy at least to have his friend by his side, even if his dog talking in an Aussie accent took a little getting used to.

"Reckon this is the right gaff though," Chimp went on.

Fergus nodded. Because he was pretty sure that the only person who could live in such an odd place was a magician.

And, as far as he knew, the only one of those in the Kingdom of Nevermore was Percy the Pretty Useless, father of none other than –

"Unlucky Luke!" exclaimed Fergus as a pale, lanky figure came bounding out of the house – yes, still with his chicken claws – tripped over the gargoyle and fell flat on his face.

"Oh, it's you!" said Luke, as he picked himself up. "I thought you were Lily."

"She's not here yet?" asked Fergus. "But I thought we were late."

"She's never on time these days," complained Luke. "Not now she's got that bike. She's practising whenever she can sneak away from the castle. Waldorf's always trying to catch her out. She can do bunny hops now! But listen, we've got news about your dad . . ."

"You're here!" hailed a familiar voice, aboard a familiar vehicle that came to a neat stop just inches from Fergus's feet. But if this really was Princess Lily, then where was her enormous dress and the mismatched wellies? And why was she wearing a motorbike helmet?

"Took your advice," said the girl, pulling the heavy hat off her head to reveal she was, despite first appearances, still a princess. "Borrowed some of Waldorf's hand-me-downs. Not that he'd ever hand anything down to me, just throw it in the bin."

"Nice work," admitted Fergus, because there was no arguing that the breeches were far better for riding in than her puffy skirts.

NO CYCLING

"Shame about the helmet," added Lily, tapping it. "But this is all I could find, what with the cycling ban. It belongs to one of the Knights of No Nonsense. He's off with chicken pox so I reckon I've got at least another week before I have to sneak it back."

"The knights wear motorbike helmets?" asked Fergus.

"Well, seeing as they ride motorbikes that would make sense," Lily pointed out.

"Weird," said Fergus.

"Better than nothing," said Chimp.

"Besides, I needed a helmet where I was going. That's why I was late today. I've narrowed down where your dad could be to three places."

"Let's go!" yelled Fergus.

"Hold your horses!" said Lily. "Or your handlebars, anyway. I've just checked out the Dungeon of Despair and the Turret of Terror and there's nothing there but dust and mice."

Fergus shuddered and so did Chimp. Flying monkeys were bad enough, even stone ones, but mice? Not on your nellie!

"So what's left?" asked Fergus, expecting the Well of Everlasting Torment, or the Forest of Certain Death or something equally horrible and dangerous-sounding.

"It's terrifying . . ." said Lily.

"Tremble-making," added Luke.

"It's . . . " Lily built up to the big announcement. ". . . Cook's Pantry!"

Fergus heaved a sigh of relief. "That doesn't sound too scary," he said.

Unlucky Luke and Lily shot each other a look.

"You haven't met Cook, have you?" said Luke.

Fergus shook his head.

"Well, brace yourself," said Lily. "She's the scariest thing in the whole kingdom."

"Really?"

"Really. Cross my heart and hope to kiss Dimwit if I'm lying," said Lily.

Wow, thought Fergus. *That meant it must be true.* And given that the Kingdom of Nevermore also contained Hounds of Horribleness as well as several dragons, he realised this was going to be harder than he had hoped. But he had to do it – he needed to get his dad back home to save Carnoustie Common. He'd know exactly what to do. Dads always did. Or at least the ones in Fergus's imagination did.

"Nevermore to Fergus," yelled Lily. "Come in, Fergus!"

Fergus looked up, shook himself. He

couldn't worry about Bruce's Biscuits and the common right now. He had a job to do.

"Let's go," he said.

"Bonzer!" yelled Chimp.

"Beast!" cried Lily.

"Brilliotic!" agreed Luke.

Fergus was surprised to hear that word, but that was another thing he didn't have time to wonder about. Nope, right now they had a dad to rescue, and by the sound of it, from a woman who made Cruella de Vil look like a puppy dog.

Cook's Kitchen

"Shhhhh," whispered Lily, as they crept down the corridor.

"Keep it zipped," added Luke, although the sound of his chicken claws tapping on the stone floor was hardly stealthy, and Fergus was pretty sure any passing palace guard would be able to hear his own heart it was hammering so loud.

The gang rounded the corner, backs against the wall, as Princess Lily peered behind a heavy wooden door, out of which came a tangled and not at all tantalising whiff of fish, drain cleaner and something that Fergus thought smelled like disappointment.

"Yup, this is the kitchen, all right," said Luke. "Serving up the worst food in five kingdoms."

Lily giggled. "You're lucky the coast is clear," she said. "Or Cook would have your guts for garters . . . or pudding, more like."

"Yuck," said Fergus.

"You'd better believe it," said Lily. "Now come on, we've got to search the meat locker before she comes back."

KEEP OUT

BY ORDER
OF COOK

"The meat locker?" asked Chimp excitedly.

"Oh yes," said Lily. "It's a massive room where Cook keeps all the sausages and hams and, well, maybe a very live grown-up man."

"But why in the meat locker?" asked Fergus.

"Because if you knew Cook," said Lily, "you'd know why it was safer than any locked dungeon."

Fergus shivered. Chimp salivated at the thought of sausages. And all four of them tiptoed towards their destination.

"Right, this is it," said Lily as they arrived at the grey metal door. "Give me a hand, Luke. Or should I say paw?"

Fergus looked at the ends of his friend's arms. Lily hadn't been lying. In all the excitement he hadn't noticed them earlier, but there, instead of

fingers, were fat hairy pads, like a bear's.
"Your dad?" Fergus asked Luke.

"One day he'll crack it again," Luke
shrugged.

"Come on," said Lily. "Heave!"

They heaved, and heaved, until finally
the metal shuddered and groaned on its
pulley and opened to reveal . . .

Nothing.

Well, not nothing. There were three pheasants hanging upside-down by their legs, and a very cross cat that shot between Lily's legs and into a corner where it cowered.

"Suet!" said Lily. "That's where you got to!"

"Suet?" whimpered Chimp, cowering behind Fergus. He liked cats even less than mice and monkeys.

"Suet?" asked Fergus.

"The kitchen kitten!" said Lily. "Well, cat now. Aren't you, kitty? Percy magicked him up the day Luke was born."

A magic kitten? thought Fergus. He knelt down and held his hand out carefully to the cat, who pushed its nose forward just a fraction. But before Fergus could inch any further, a massive jet of sludge hit Suet on the bottom, sending him howling damply out of the door and down the corridor.

"Waldorf?" yelled Lily, all thoughts of hiding from Cook forgotten now.

Fergus watched as Princess Lily's ghastly twin brother appeared from behind a pillar. "Got it in one," he said. "Rather like my shot at that idiotic cat."

"That cat's not an idiot," blurted

Fergus. "He's –" but he stopped. Because Fergus didn't know what he was. Or if he was even a he.

"Anyway, the cat's not who we're after," said Waldorf, "is it?"

His sidekick Dimmock, who had been lurking in the shadows, stepped forward and shook his head.

"We're after someone who's been up to no good, aren't we?"

Dimmock nodded this time.

"Someone who's been dressing up in boys' clothes and riding an illegal bicycle."

Dimmock nodded again.

"Someone like . . ."

Waldorf raised his sludge gun and aimed it right at his sister.

"Me?" asked Lily, bracing herself.

Fergus narrowed his eyes. "You'll have to hit me first," he said, stepping in front of her.

"Oi!" hissed Lily. "Just because I'm a girl doesn't mean I need protecting."

"I'm not doing it because you're a girl," whispered Fergus. "I'm doing it because you're my friend."

"Oh, that's okay then,' said Lily. 'Go ahead."

Fergus closed his eyes and steeled himself for the sludge attack. But, just as he was expecting a shot of green custardy slime to explode against his t-shirt, he felt the ground begin to shudder.

He opened his eyes again to find that Waldorf had dropped the gun and turned as pale as Luke.

"Is that an … earthquake?" whimpered Chimp.

Lily shook her head. "Way worse than an earthquake," she said.

"Or a volcano," added Luke.

"Or a vat of boiling oil infested by boy-eating sharks," said Waldorf, who had clearly pondered such things at length.

"That –" said Lily as the sound got louder and louder and nearer and nearer – "is Cook. Scram!"

Waldorf and Dimwit skedaddled one way, while Luke and Lily scooted the other, Fergus and Chimp following them a few steps behind.

"Get on your bike," yelled Lily. "And get out of here!"

"I will," panted Fergus. "But I'm coming back."

"When?" asked Lily.

"Soon," he replied as he yanked out his bike from the chicken shed. "Sooner than soon."

"Beast!" said Lily. "And don't worry about Suet, I know what you're thinking, and I've got your back."

"You've what?" asked Fergus who had no idea what she was talking about. What WAS he thinking? And what did she mean by "got your back"?

"I'm behind you," said Lily. Fergus still looked baffled – she was in front of him at the moment. "I'm with you?" she tried before eventually just saying it like it is. "I'm your friend."

"Me too," said Luke who had hopped on the back of Lily's bike for a croggy.

"Me three," said Chimp. "But we'll all of us be dead meat instead of mates if we don't get out of here!"

Fergus didn't need to be told a second time, and with Chimp sat on the handlebars, he started pedalling as fast as he could, building up speed until he could let go, spin back and . . .

SCREEECH!

Fergus slammed on his brakes and pulled up hard on Carnoustie Common.

He was safe. Home and dry.

Except . . .

"We failed, Chimp," he said. "We didn't get Dad. We didn't even FIND Dad."

He looked at his dog, who was idly sniffing a crisp packet. "Chimp?"

Chimp looked up and gave him a bark.

"Of course," muttered Fergus grumpily. "No magic here. Just hard work."

But as soon as he said the words, it came to him. He knew how they'd do it – how they'd get the rest of the signatures for the petition: hard work.

Loads of people had come to the shop to put their names down, but not everyone could get out of their houses. Over the road from the park was an old people's home and Fergus bet they'd all rather look at Carnoustie Common than a biscuit factory belching out smoke all day.

That was it.

"Come on, boy!" he called to Chimp. "We've got work to do. And so have the rest of the team. After all, that's what friends are for."

And so, barely recovered from the chase with Cook, but fired up with enthusiasm, Fergus sped home to start the ball rolling.

The Petition

Fergus, Daisy, Minnie, Calamity and Chimp made for an odd fivesome knocking on the door of Withering Heights Retirement Home. But their smiles and determination more than made up for their oily fingers and muddy knees (and paws).

"Who is it?" asked an elderly voice inside.

Fergus recognised her instantly.

"It's me, Mrs Muldoon."

"Who's me?" replied the old lady.

"Fergus," said Fergus. "Fergus Hamilton. My grandpa's called Hercules. I think you –"

But no sooner than Fergus mentioned the name Hercules, the door was flung open.

"Och, Herc!" cried the old lady with delight. "Such a charmer. Such a champion! If I were five years younger . . ."

More like twenty-five, thought Fergus. But he didn't say it. Nor did he say how mad it was that the lady who seemed to be running the old people's home was older than half the residents.

"Now," said Mrs Muldoon, gripping Fergus's small hand in her own bony one. "Any friend of Herc is a friend of mine. So how can I help you?"

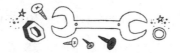

As soon as they heard about the plans for the factory, the residents were queuing to sign the petition.

"Biscuits, indeed," said Colonel Nidgett. "Carrots, that's what they need. Help you see in the dark, you know."

"Well, I do like a nice Rich Tea," said Mrs Bottomley, "but not as much as I like to watch the ducks and the dogs and the kiddies having fun."

They weren't the only two. All in all the team got thirty-seven signatures. Then, on Mr Groutley's advice (who used to be a nurse), they tried the hospital on the other side of the park and got an amazing one hundred and ninety-two signatures there.

"We've done it!" cried Daisy when they burst back through the shop door.

"We have." Fergus grinned.

Grandpa Herc scrolled through the pages and pages of names and good wishes.

"By jinks," he said. "You really have." He looked at them all with eyes glittering with tears of happiness. "That is some of the best team work I've witnessed.

I've never been prouder. Not even when you got through to Districts."

Fergus beamed. "Let's hope Mr McGovern agrees," he said.

Grandpa nodded, wiping his eyes hastily. "Aye. Hope. That's what we've got to do now. Hope as hard as you can. And then some."

So hope Fergus did. He hoped all through tea, even though it was beetroot salad. He hoped while he was brushing his teeth. He hoped before he fell asleep and he hoped when he woke up again. And then he hoped all the way to the town hall, up the steps and into Malky McGovern's office.

"Well, I'll be blown," said Malky, gazing at the petition and the jar of money. His eyes were sparkling just like Grandpa's had.

"A thing of wonder, isn't it?" said Grandpa.

"Aye," said Malky, nodding slowly. "That it is. A thing of wonder."

"So?" asked Fergus, unable to contain his excitement any longer. "Have we done enough? Have we collected enough signatures? Have we got enough money?"

Malky laughed. "Sonny, you'd need another fifty thousand pounds to have enough money to beat Bruce's Biscuits –"

"What?" yelped Fergus, feeling his heart plummet like a stone dropped in a pond. "You said it was a thing of wonder! You said –"

"I hadn't finished what I was saying, actually," said Malky. "No, you don't have enough money to buy the land. But you don't need to. You have the support of the community. They've made it clear what they want, and that's enough for me. We won't be selling the land off at the moment to anyone for any amount of money."

Fergus felt the stone lift and his heart with it until he was sure he was soaring above them all, he was so happy.

"Really?"

"Really. It won't be the end of it, mind. I'm sure old Bruce will put up a fight in the long run. But you can keep the park for now. And if you can build a decent track on it, your case will be even better."

"But we don't have any money to do that!" wailed Fergus.

"Yes, you do," said Malky McGovern, and he pushed the jar back across his desk. "You've got, what, seven hundred pounds?"

"Seven hundred and eighty-three

pounds and forty-two pence," said Fergus, not quite believing what he was seeing. "To be precise."

"So there you go," said Malky. "That'll build you something, anyway."

"I can't thank you enough, Malky," said Grandpa, who had finally found his voice.

"No, it's me who should be thanking you. It's a good thing your boy's done."

"Not just Fergus," said Grandpa. "The whole team. The whole community, in fact."

"Aye. And that's what counts, eh? Community."

Grandpa nodded, his eyes glittery again.

"Och, you're not going to cry again, are you?" asked Fergus. "We did it. We won! It's over."

Grandpa shook his head. "That we did," he laughed. "But over? You must be joking, sonny. Now comes the hard part."

Grandpa wasn't joking. Fergus didn't think he'd ever worked harder than he did that week. Together with Daisy and the rest of the team, as well as everyone who'd helped with the campaign – from Mrs MacCafferty to Jambo Patterson himself – Fergus found himself running home from school to help clear and dig and flatten, and finally spread out what looked pretty much like a load of old ash from the fire.

"What IS this stuff?" he asked, as they stood back and surveyed their hard work. "It doesn't look like any track I've ever seen." It certainly didn't look like the one at Middlebank, that was for sure.

"Don't you know?" said Daisy, who clearly did, and was clearly about to tell him. "It's cinders."

"All the old races were on cinder tracks," added Grandpa. "It's a great surface to practise on."

"Plus it's a whole lot cheaper and quicker than tarmac," smiled Jambo.

"Aye," laughed Grandpa. "That an' all."

"Looks like a cat litter tray," sneered a familiar voice.

"Wesley," sighed Fergus, seeing the faces of his arch-enemy and his sidekick Dermot Eggs sneering at him from the sidelines.

"Suits you," continued Wesley. "Seeing as you're all a bit POO!"

"Are not!" yelled Daisy and Fergus together.

"Are!" insisted Wesley.

"Yeah, are!" added Dermot.

"That's quite enough!" interrupted Grandpa. "This is supposed to be about community spirit, not name-calling."

"He wouldn't know anything about that," said Daisy.

"Whatever," replied Wesley, "but I know one thing: even with a new track you're still a loser, Hamilton. Have you forgotten about our little bet? Time's up. Me and you, here, tomorrow."

"You're on," said Fergus before he could stop himself.

"But we haven't tested it out yet!" warned Daisy.

"Well, that *will* make it a fairer race," Jambo pointed out. "And the publicity would be grand, don't you think, Herc? A lovely cover for the May Day edition of the paper."

Grandpa frowned at Fergus, but Fergus knew he wasn't going to get in the way of publicity.

"Aye, you're on," Grandpa said finally. "Could be a chance to nab a sponsor, after all. A race it is. Tomorrow at ten. You bring the photographer, Jambo, I'll bring the biscuits."

"But not Bruce's, mind," said Jambo.

"Why don't I make some?" said Mum, who seemed to have appeared out of nowhere.

Jambo smiled at her, "Well that'd be just dandy, Mrs Hamilton."

"Och, call me Jeanie," said Mum.

"Jeanie it is." Mum grinned. Fergus pulled a face.

"Er, can we go now? I've got a race in the morning, after all."

Mum nodded. "Aye, sorry, Fergie. Time for tea, eh?"

Jambo smiled. "See you tomorrow, Jeanie. And you, Fergus," he added hurriedly. "Show us what you're made of."

Fergus nodded enthusiastically. He would, he would show Wesley and all of them exactly what he was made of.

But as he lay in bed that night, Fergus felt his head fill with a hundred questions.

What if he couldn't ride on cinders?

What if he made a fool of himself falling off?

What if the whole thing had been a massive mistake?

Tomorrow was D-Day. Not just for him, for the whole community. He had to show them all their donations and support had been worth it. He had to prove HE was worth it.

Right then, just a small boy wrapped in a spotty duvet, Fergus wasn't at all sure he was worth it.

The Starting Line

The morning dawned hazy and bright, with a low cloud of mist hanging over Carnoustie Common as if it was shrouded in clouds, like a fairytale castle.

"It'll lift by ten," promised Grandpa, as he, Fergus and Chimp stood surveying the dark cinder track that ran round the park like a black ribbon. "The sun will push through and you'll do the same, sonny, I can feel it in my bones."

Fergus wasn't too convinced of Grandpa's fortune-telling skills – he'd once felt it in his bones that Rangers were going to win the double and they lost 5-0. But he'd take all the hope he could get, which meant he had Grandpa's bones, his Mum's big lipsticky kiss as she'd sent them off, and Chimp's lucky toy monkey that he'd dropped soggily onto Fergus's face to wake him up.

"Hey!" Fergus felt a small fist bump his arm.

"Ow!" he exclaimed.

"Pinch and a punch for first day of the month!" Daisy grinned. "It's for good luck."

"That's four-leaf clovers," Fergus pointed out.

"Or seagulls pooing on you, though why that would be good luck is anyone's guess."

"True," said Daisy. "My mum once wanted me to use an umbrella on the beach just in case I got bombarded." She shook her head at the memory, then shook herself back to the here and now. "You ready, then?"

Fergus stretched and wriggled, checking his muscles and warming them up. "As I'll ever be."

"Beast!" replied Daisy. "Because here comes your opposition."

Fergus followed her gaze across the park to see Wesley Wallace wheeling his bike towards them, followed by a small crowd of people, some in racing gear, some in normal clothes, but all wearing Wallace's Winners caps and scarves in their official team colours and carrying flags that Fergus knew without looking would say "Sponsored by Bruce's Biscuits".

"Who's that with him?" asked Calamity.

"Dermot," said Daisy, squinting. "Choppy. The rest of the team. I don't know the rest."

"Probably people from the biscuit factory."

"Yeah." Daisy snorted. "Bet old Brian Bruce had to pay them extra to show up. That's the only reason Belinda Bruce is on Wallace's Winners, I reckon."

Fergus stared at the massive factory gang with their placards protesting the council's decision about the park, then glanced round at his own back-up and wondered if he should have thought of something like that. Because apart from Grandpa and Chimp, only Jambo had arrived, along with his photographer, and Jambo was the race official so he didn't really count.

"There'll be more soon," said Daisy, reading his thoughts.

Fergus checked his watch. "Well, they'd better get a shimmy on," he said. "Race starts in two minutes."

But by the time Fergus and Wesley lined up at the start, only a few kids from school and Fergus's mum had joined his supporters. She had brought homemade cookies, which Jambo and the others were tucking into happily.

Fergus's tummy rumbled as he wondered if they were cherry or chocolate chip. He'd been too shaky to eat a big breakfast, though Grandpa had forced him to have some toast and a banana for energy. He didn't have time to think about chocolate chip anything now.

"Ready, sonny?" asked Grandpa.

Fergus nodded, even though he felt far from ready. In fact, he felt more like cycling off in the other direction entirely. But it wasn't just his reputation at stake, it was his whole team's, and everyone who'd helped to build the track, so he had a job to do, and a big one at that.

"You know the score," said Grandpa. "Focus on the finish line."

"Too right," added Daisy.

"Good luck, Fergie." Minnie patted him on the back.

"Yeah, do it for the team." Calamity patted him too, almost sending him flying. "Oops!" he said.

Fergus righted himself. "S'okay," he said. "And I will, I'll do it for all of us."

Even though "all of us" wasn't looking like a whole huge lot compared to Wesley's loud crowd, who were waving rattles and flags and yelling "cheers" as they chinked cans of fizzy pop together.

"Ignore them," said Grandpa. "Eyes on the prize, remember."

"Yeah, don't let those losers distract you."

"I won't," said Fergus.

But as Jambo raised the starting flag, Fergus felt more sure than ever that the prize was out of his grasp, and the only loser round here might just be him.

Head to Head

"On your marks!" cried Jambo.

Fergus leaned forward over the handlebars. Wesley leaned sideways.

"Fat chance," he sneered. "Have fun breathing in my dust."

Fergus gritted his teeth.

But Wesley wasn't finished. "I'm the fastest in the county and you know it," he continued. "I beat you in the Great Cycle Challenge, I'm going to beat you in the Districts, but first, I'll beat you today."

"Get set!" Jambo yelled.

"It's not all about speed," hissed Fergus. "What about patience? And skill?"

"WhatEVER, loser." Wesley laughed and leaned back into his place.

Fergus tried to shake the words out of his head. He was not going to fall behind, he just wasn't. Wesley might be right about being the fastest in the county, but Fergus was going to give him a run for his money at least. He placed his right foot on the pedal and took a deep breath.

"GO!" Jambo shouted, waving the flag down with a flourish.

And with that, Fergus pushed down hard and flew forward over the cinders for the very first time.

Woah! It WAS different. It was good, hard and fast and, best of all, fun!

He pushed down and down, each time building up speed, each time getting further towards the finish.

But someone else was building speed too.

Wesley kept pace with Fergus wheel spin for wheel spin. There wasn't a hair's breadth between the pair as they rounded the first corner and headed out along the long straight, away from their cheering teams and out of earshot of their coachs' advice.

"Come on," Fergus said to himself, trying to think what Grandpa would tell him to do right now. "Give it some welly!" So he gave it some welly, nudging out in front of Wesley by a few inches. But Wesley sensed it before he saw it and gave it more.

The pair rounded the far bend and hit the home straight neck and neck.

And that's when it happened.

Fergus would have rubbed his eyes if he'd been able to take his hands off the handlebars, because he couldn't quite believe what he was seeing. Or hearing.

"Come on, Fergie!" yelled a voice. But it wasn't Grandpa, or Daisy, or Mum or anyone he knew that well – it was the woman who ran the greengrocer's on the corner who'd given them a few pounds towards the track.

"You can do it, our Fergus!" shouted someone else. This time it was Mr Lomax who'd helped pick up litter from the common before the diggers came in.

One by one more voices joined in – Mrs MacCafferty, Colonel Nidgett from his wheelchair, even Malky McGovern from the council – until the individual cheers became a cacophony of encouragement, willing Fergus on and on towards the finish line.

These people all believe in me! thought Fergus. But what was it Grandpa said? Yes, that was it: "You've got to believe in yourself, too."

He did believe, he believed he could do it. So what if he was racing against Wesley Wallace, the fastest boy in the county? So what if this was a new track and he'd not had time to practise? And so what if his dad wasn't here to see him race – all these other people were, and in the middle of them all were Mum, Grandpa and Chimp, who were the best family he could have wished for. With that Fergus dug deep and found that last burst of energy he was looking for. Not much, but enough to nudge him an inch ahead of Wesley, then four, then eight, until by the time he crossed the finishing line, there was a whole wheel width between them.

Fergus screeched to a halt sending
a cloud of ash up into Wesley's face.
"Sorry," he said quickly.

Wesley coughed and spat blackly onto the ground. "It was this stupid track," he spluttered. "That's all. I'll still beat you next month, you'll see."

Fergus was sorry he'd made Wesley eat ashes, but only a tiny bit, because as his old friends and new ones came to hug him and clap him and slap him on the back, he knew this wasn't just a win for him, but for everyone who lived round Carnoustie Common who'd fought to save it, and, by doing so, given the team a fighting chance for a real future.

A New Number One

"I hereby declare Fergus Hamilton the inaugural winner of the Carnoustie Cinder Sprint," announced Jambo happily, handing Fergus a box of chocolates as a prize. "I'd have got a trophy done, but there wasn't the time," he whispered. "Next year, though, eh?"

Fergus laughed, and held the chocs high in the air anyway, sending the crowd into another rousing cheer.

"But that's not all," said Jambo, addressing the crowd again. "I'm also delighted to be the one to hand over this."

He held a fat parcel out to Fergus, wrapped in brown paper and tied with string.

"Here," said Daisy. "I'll mind the chocs while you unwrap it."

Fergus grinned. "Okay," he said. "But only have a few, and none for Chimp, mind!"

"Promise," said Daisy. Though it came out more like "Prrgghhmmmmllp" as she was already chewing on a chocolate mint toffee.

Fergus took the parcel in his hands, and pulled at the string bow, then peeled off the sticky tape piece by piece until he could fold out the paper and see what was inside.

"Seriously?" he asked, looking back at Jambo.

"Seriously!" Jambo exclaimed. "But don't look at me, this isn't my doing."

Fergus turned to Grandpa and gave him a smile so big he thought his face might crack. Inside the parcel were brand new jerseys, all in red and yellow, and all emblazoned with the same slogan on the back: "Sponsored by Herc's Hand-Me-Downs".

"But – but how can you afford it?" he asked.

"Well," began Grandpa, "all that old junk at the back of the shop turned out to be worth more than I thought."

"And the publicity from the campaign made a difference," added Jambo.

"Aye," agreed Grandpa. "While you were at school or down here working all week, people were queuing at the shop to get their bikes fixed or buy new ones."

"So it's not just you beating Wesley," said Jambo. "We're all giving old Choppy Wallace something to think about."

"Not everyone wants new all the time," said Mum. "Some of us appreciate the already-loved things in life."

"Never a truer word," said Jambo, smiling at her.

Mum giggled. Fergus groaned. Parents were just so totally embarrassing. He turned back to survey the scene instead.

This was a moment he wanted to savour: a new track, new kit and a brilliant team, too. But more than that, tens, even hundreds of people all wanting them to be a success. And that was more than Wesley and his lot could dream of, which was probably why they'd slunk off so quickly after the race.

That night Fergus lay in bed replaying the voices that had called out to him during the race:

"Keep going, kid!" from Julie Gilhoolie the lollipop lady.

"You can do it," from Mr Miggins who lived above the launderette.

"That's very good, Fergus," from Mrs Devlin, Daisy's mum – even if she had been hiding behind Mr Devlin in terror at the time.

But he'd heard other voices in his head too: Lily telling him to "Keep at it!" Unlucky Luke yelling, "Way to go, Fergus!" as he danced on his chicken feet. And, strangest of all, a soft Scots accent he'd never heard before, telling him he was always right there with him, however far away he might seem.

It was his Dad. Fergus just knew it. Maybe he hadn't been able to help Fergus save the common, but Fergus could still hear his voice, encouraging him, from wherever he was.

Fergus thought about the kitchen in Nevermore, and what he'd learned from his newfound friends. And that's when the idea came to him. Hadn't Daisy said Luke had got Suet as a kitten? And how old was Luke? Nine. Nine years old, the same as Fergus. And how long had dad been missing? Nine years. Plus Luke's dad Percy could turn humans into animals and back again, or at least he used to be able to. Which could mean . . .

By JINKS! thought Fergus. It was a crazy idea but . . . could it be that his dad had been turned into a cat? He glanced down at Chimp. Now that was going to be tough news to break. Then he smiled to himself. Yup, living in two parallel universes could be tough at times, but it could be really rewarding too. Friends and family, that was all that mattered, after all. And he had both, in both worlds, in abundance. He had a real community.

And with that thought slipping down inside him like warm syrup on porridge, Fergus finally fell asleep.

Joanna Nadin is the author of more than fifty books for children and teenagers, including the bestselling Rachel Riley Diaries and the award-winning Penny Dreadful series. Amongst other accolades she has been nominated for the Carnegie Medal and shortlisted for the Roald Dahl Funny Prize, and is the winner of the Fantastic Book Award, Highland Book Award and the Surrey Book Award. Joanna has been a journalist and adviser to the Prime Minister, and now teaches creative writing at Bath Spa University. She lives in Bath and loves to ride her rickety bicycle, but doesn't manage to go very fast. And she never, ever back-pedals . . .

Sir Chris Hoy MBE, won his first Olympic gold medal in Athens 2004. Four years later in Beijing he became the first Briton since 1908 to win three gold medals in a single Olympic Games. In 2012, Chris won two gold medals at his home Olympics in London, becoming Britain's most successful Olympian with six gold medals and one silver. Sir Chris also won eleven World titles and two Commonwealth Games gold medals. In December 2008, Chris was voted BBC Sports Personality of the Year, and he received a Knighthood in the 2009 New Year Honours List. Sir Chris retired as a professional competitive cyclist in early 2013; he still rides almost daily. He lives in Manchester with his wife and son.

The

FLYING FERGUS

series

Available now

The Best Birthday Bike

The Great Cycle Challenge

The Big Biscuit Bike Off

and coming soon

The Championship Cheats

Catch up with Fergus and his friends in the fourth thrilling adventure, when they face
THE CHAMPIONSHIP CHEATS

The District Championships are finally here but are the Hercules' Hopefuls bikes good enough against the other teams' flashy state-of-the-art cycles? Choppy Wallace offers the whole team brand-new Sullivan Swifts – the bike of Fergus's dreams! But is it a trick?